Postman Pat
Goes t

Story by **John Cunliffe**   Pictures by **Joan Hickson**
From the original Television designs by **Ivor Wood**

Hippo

Scholastic Children's Books
Commonwealth House, 1-19 New Oxford Street
London WC1A 1NU

A division of Scholastic Publications Ltd
London ~ New York ~ Toronto ~ Sydney ~ Auckland

First published in the UK by Scholastic Children's Books 1989
This edition published in 1996
Text copyright © John Cunliffe 1989 and 1993
Illustrations copyright © Scholastic Publications Ltd
and Woodland Animations Ltd 1989

A longer version of this story has been previously published as a Handy Hippo

ISBN 0 590 54139 0

10 9 8 7 6 5 4 3 2 1

Typeset by Rapid Reprographics Ltd
Printed in Italy by L.E.G.O. S.p.A.

John Cunliffe has asserted his moral right to be identified as the author of this
work in accordance with the Copyright, Design and Patents Act, 1988.

"What's all this," said Mrs Goggins, "about you going to London?"

"Oh, it's true enough," said Pat. "I'll be down there for a week — at the end of May."

"Whatever for, Pat? Isn't Greendale good enough for you?"

"My goodness," Pat laughed, "Greendale's certainly good enough for me. There's no better place in all the world. But I have to go to London, just for a week. The country postmen have to spend a week in town, and the town postmen have to spend a week in the country."

"Funny idea," said Mrs Goggins. "What a muddle there'll be. I don't know who will get the most mixed up."

"Oh, I don't know," said Pat. "It might be fun."

"Well, they'd better not send me to London, that's all I can say," said Mrs Goggins.

"You don't know what you might be missing," said Pat.

"Aunt Lucy went to London, once,"
said Mrs Goggins, "and she lost her purse."

7

"Your aunt Lucy once lost a *cow*, in Greendale," said Pat, laughing. "And that was nobody's fault but her own!"

"And nobody ever knew how it managed to turn up in the Reverend Timms' garden," said Mrs Goggins.

"He was very nice about it," said Pat,
"considering that it ate a row of his lettuces."
Pat was on his way.

9

The time came for Pat to go to London. The big inter-city train whisked Pat away. Away it took him, miles and miles.

Past farms, and fields, and motorways, and churches, and villages, and towns, and factories, and canals, and houses, and schools, and more houses, and trees, and hills, and valleys, and on, and on, and on!

Pat looked out of the window.

"Bless me," he said to himself. "What a big place the world is. And what a lot of people! And they all get letters. There must be hundreds and hundreds of postmen. I wonder if any of them have a cat like Jess."

When Pat arrived, he saw thousands of people, and they all seemed to be in a hurry. What should he do now? Which way should he go?

He saw a man, holding a piece of card in front of him. What did it say?

POST OFFICE STAFF — MEETING POINT
Post office? Where? Oh! STAFF. Perhaps this man was...? Pat went up to him.

"Excuse me. Are you from the Post Office? Are you..."

"That's right, mate. Hang on a mo... You on my list? ...Name?"

"Um...er...Pat."

"Pat who?"

"Pat Clifton. From Greendale."

"Gotcher. My name's Fred. I'll run you down to the canteen for a cuppa'. Okay?"

There was a minibus full of postmen in the goods-yard. Fred flung the doors open, and Pat got in.

They were off at speed through the streets of London, hanging on for dear life. Black taxis and big red London buses zoomed past them. What a noisy, smelly place London was!

When they arrived at the Post Office building, they went into a huge dining hall, where hundreds of people were having meals and drinks.

"Just look!" said Pat. "There are more postwomen than postmen."

"And they're a great bunch!" said Fred.

"We could do with a few of them in Pencaster," said Pat.

There were so many things to do and see in London, that Pat was glad when Fred said, "Right, mates, knocking-off time. I'll run you round to the hotel."

They were all so tired that they slept soundly.

The next day, Fred came for them all very early, and took them racing off in the minibus.

"Time to do some work, now!" shouted Fred, cheerfully.

He dropped each of them at a different post office.

"We'll get lost!" said Pat.

"Don't worry," said Fred. "You'll be going out with somebody who knows the ropes."

"I wish I had Jess and my van with me," thought Pat.

But when Pat met Val, he forgot all about Jess and his van.

"She'll look after you," said Fred. "You'll have a good laugh with Val. Ta ra!"

With a big smile, Val nearly shook Pat's hand off. She seemed to find everything a big joke.

"Hi!" she said. "Good to see ya! Welcome to Happy Hampstead! I hope you're good on hills? Let's go, Pat!"

There were more letters in the sorting office than Pat had ever seen all at once. It seemed as if all the world's letters had arrived in Hampstead that day.

"It's nothing," said Val. "We'll soon shift this lot."

Val sorted the letters at an amazing speed.

"I'm not much of a help, am I?" said Pat.

"You'll be a great help," said Val. "You can carry the parcels. I hate them blessed parcels, I really do."

Off they went. Up stairs and down
stairs in the flats, and down again to
basements, half under the ground. In and
out of garden gates. Down back alleys, into
yards, and in and out of squares.

21

Dogs barked and snapped at them.
People pushed by them in their hurry. Cars,
and taxis, and buses, and lorries made a
roaring and a smell all day.

23

Pat's legs began to ache. His back began
to ache. He thought of his van, with Jess
sitting in his basket. But Val kept him
smiling. She told him stories about the
people and the places they saw. She told
him about her home in Jamaica.

They called at the church. He half
expected to see the Reverend Timms come
smiling out to meet them. But it was a
young man with red hair who met them at
the door, and he was carrying a guitar.

Their bags were empty at last.

"Thank goodness," said Pat.

"We have to go back for another lot, now!" said Val, "but we'll stop for a coffee, first."

"Great!" said Pat.

While they were doing their second delivery, Pat told Val all about Greendale. Her eyes grew big and round.

"I'd sure like to come and see it," she said.

As the week went on, Pat could be more help to Val. He began to know his way about.

"I'll be sorry to see you go," she said. "You're just getting to be useful."

On Wednesday, after their work was done, Val took Pat to meet her family. Val's husband cooked a Jamaican meal. Pat loved it.

"You'll have to give me the recipe," he said. "I'll make some of this for Sara and Julian."

On Thursday, Pat took them all for a meal at a Chinese restaurant.

And on Friday, Val's friend, Dipali, made them a hot curry. Then they went to hear a steel band at the church hall.

Saturday was a day off. Pat saw Buckingham Palace, the Tower of London, Piccadilly Circus, and London Zoo. He sent postcards to Sara and Julian, and bought presents for them. Then it was time to pack up and catch the tube to Euston station.

Fred and Val and lots of other Post Office people came to see him off.

Everyone shook hands, and said, "Thanks for a great week," and Val promised to come and see Pat in Greendale.

The train soon got up speed. There was more and more green between the houses and factories. Pat saw a grassy hill, with trees on the top and sheep all over it. Then he knew how much he had missed Greendale.

And it didn't seem long before the voice on the speakers was saying, "We are now arriving at Pencaster. All change for trains to Windermere. Pencaster!" and Pat was getting out on to the windy platform of Pencaster station, and giving Sara and Julian a hug.

They asked him so many questions about his week in London that he felt almost as muddled as the day he arrived at Euston and stood in the middle of the great crowd of people.

"I'll tell you all about it," he said; "tomorrow."

Ted was waiting in his Land-rover, and he drove them home to Greendale.

"It's good to be back," said Pat.

But, the next Saturday afternoon, he took Sara and Julian to Lancaster for a Chinese meal.